This book belongs to

....

LADYBIRD BOOKS

UK | USA | Canada | Ireland | Australia | India | New Zealand | South Africa

Ladybird Books is part of the Penguin Random House group of companies
whose addresses can be found at global.penguinrandomhouse.com.

www.penguin.co.uk   www.puffin.co.uk   www.ladybird.co.uk

Penguin
Random House
UK

First published 2023
001

Licensed by

Printed in China

The authorized representative in the EEA is Penguin Random House Ireland,
Morrison Chambers, 32 Nassau Street, Dublin D02 YH68

A CIP catalogue record for this book is available from the British Library

ISBN: 978-0-241-60698-8

All correspondence to:
Ladybird Books, Penguin Random House Children's
One Embassy Gardens, 8 Viaduct Gardens, London SW11 7BW

Peppa's DINOSAUR Party

Peppa and George were visiting Granny and Grandpa Pig.

"Grandpa!" cheered Peppa.

"Hello, Peppa. Hello, George," said Grandpa Pig.

"Dine-saw! *Grrrr!*" said George, roaring.
"And hello to you, too, Mr Dinosaur,"
said Grandpa Pig, chuckling.

Grrrr!

Suddenly, there was a loud, "*ROOOOARRR!*"
"ARGHHH!" shouted Grandpa Pig, leaping up into the air.
Granny Pig was dressed as a dinosaur!

"My goodness, Granny Pig," said Grandpa Pig. "You gave me a shock."
"Sorry," said Granny Pig. "I'm having a Dinosaur Day today!"

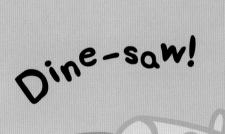

Dine-saw!

Granny Pig explained that her friends were coming round to pretend it was the time of the dinosaurs. "It's called a historical re-enactment," she said. "Sounds like a party," said Grandpa Pig.

"It's *not* a party," said Granny Pig. "It's very serious. I am dressed as a tyrannosaurus." She gave Peppa and George their costumes. "Peppa is an allosaurus, and George is a stegosaurus."

Ooooooh!

Just then, Grandad Dog arrived in his tow truck. *Beep! Beep!*
"*Grrrr!*" he growled. "Hello, everyone."
"What are you supposed to be?" asked Grandpa Pig.
"I'm a triceratops," said Grandad Dog proudly.
Peppa and George looked at the big purple dinosaur on the
back of the tow truck and wondered what it was.

Beep!
Beep!

The purple dinosaur rose up into the air . . .
"Hello!" called Granny Sheep and Granny Wolf
from underneath it. "*Grrrr!*"
"Ahh," said Grandpa Pig. "A brontosaurus."
"Actually," said Granny Pig, "this is an
apatosaurus."
"Wonderful," said Grandpa Pig. "I'll pop the
kettle on."

Grrrr!

The dinosaurs followed Granny Pig to the back garden . . .
"This is how the world looked a long time ago when there were dinosaurs," she told them.
"Let's pretend we were there," said Grandad Dog.
"What do we do?" asked Peppa.
"Stomp and roar!" said Grandad Dog.

STOMP!

ROAR!

STOMP!

"I see the party's started," said Grandpa Pig, bringing out the tea. "It's *not* a party," said Granny Pig.

ROAR!

Grampy Rabbit arrived. "HELLO!" he shouted. "Sorry I'm late."
"Why are you dressed as a caveman?" asked Granny Pig.
"Dinosaurs and cavemen go well together," replied
Grampy Rabbit.
Granny Pig said, "Well, actually, they didn't
live at the same time . . ."

But Grampy Rabbit wasn't listening.
"I'm good at being a caveman,"
he said.

AHHHH!

AH! AH!

AH! AH!

"I hope you don't mind," continued Grampy Rabbit,
"but I invited my daughter."
Everyone felt the ground beneath them begin to shake . . .

"HELLO!" Miss Rabbit shouted down from the top of a gigantic robot dragon.
THUMP! The dragon nearly knocked Granny and Grandpa Pig's house over!
"Oops, sorry!" cried Miss Rabbit. "It's a bit hard to control this thing!"

THUMP!

STOMP!
STOMP!

"That's a **dragon**," said Granny Pig. "Not a dinosaur!"

Grandpa Pig watched his garden shake with the stomping. "Didn't the dinosaurs die out at some point?" he grumbled. "Around 66 million years ago, when the world was hit by an asteroid," said Granny Pig.

"What's an **as-ter-oid?**" asked Peppa.
"A HUGE ball of rock floating through space," explained Grandad Dog.
"I wonder where we could get an asteroid from?" said Granny Pig.

Just then, Mr Fox arrived.
Granny Pig, Peppa and George went to meet him.
"Hello," said Mr Fox. "I heard you were having
a dinosaur party, and I thought I might be able
to sell you something. I've got rubber pterodactyls,
nodding herbivores . . ."

"We need an asteroid," said Granny Pig.
"It's like a **very** big ball," added Peppa.

Mr Fox thought for a moment. "I've got just the thing . . ."
he said, getting a deflated ball out from the back of his van.
"A beach ball?" asked Peppa.

"It's a GIANT beach ball!" announced Mr Fox as he started to inflate it. "You wait and see." *Pump! Pump! Pump!* "Oooh!" said Peppa. "It *is* GIANT!"

Pump! Pump! Pump!

"Perfect!" said Granny Pig once the beach ball was fully inflated. "This will be an excellent asteroid!"

The asteroid bounced past Granny and Grandpa Pig's house, and down the hill to the garden full of dinosaurs.

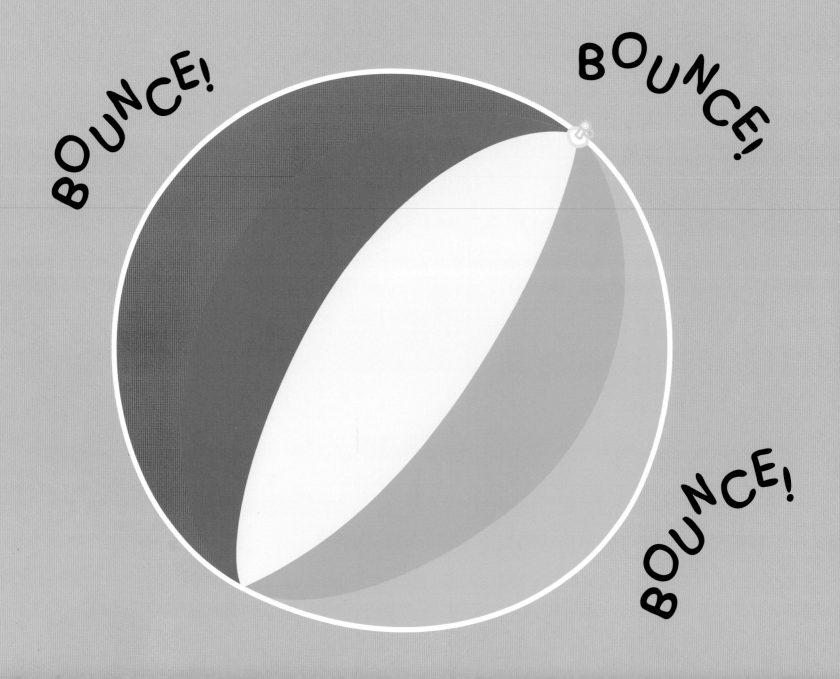

Hee! Hee! Wheee!

Peppa and George raced after it as fast as they could, followed by Granny Pig and Mr Fox.

The asteroid bounced all
around the garden . . .

BOUNCE!

BOUNCE!

BOUNCE!

bumping into the dinosaurs . . .
and even the dragon!

Mr Fox turned to Granny Pig. "You've got people in fancy dress, palm trees and a beach ball," he said. "This is an amazing beach party!"

"It's *not* a party," said Granny Pig. Mr Fox had an idea and went back to his van . . .

He came back with two big speakers on wheels. "You can't have a beach party without music," he said.

"This is the best party ever, Granny!" said Peppa. She danced and sang a song . . .

"Do the stomp. Do the dinosaur stomp!
Do the roar. Do the dinosaur roar!
Stomp! Stomp! Stomp!
Roar! Roar! Roar!
Do the dinosaur stomp, stomp, roar!"

Everyone had a fantastic time
stomping and roaring to the music.